2

Published in Great Britain in 2001 by Hodder Wayland,
an imprint of Hodder Children's Books

Text copyright © 2001 Alan Childs
Illustrations copyright © 2001 Gini Wade

The right of Alan Childs to be identified as the author of this Work
and the right of Gini Wade to be identified as the illustrator of this
Work have been asserted by them in accordance with the
Copyright, Designs and Patents Act 1988.

British Library Cataloguing in Publication Data
Childs, Alan, 1942-
Sir Walter Raleigh and the search for the City of Gold.
- (Historical storybooks)
1.Raleigh, Sir Walter, 1552?-1618 2.El Dorado
3.Historical fiction 4.Children's stories
I.Title II.Wade, Gini
823.9'14[J]

ISBN 0 7502 3764 3

Printed in Hong Kong by Wing King Tong Co. Ltd.

Hodder Children's Books,
A division of Hodder Headline Limited,
338 Euston Road,
London NW1 3BH

Sir Walter Raleigh

And the Search for the City of Gold

Alan Childs

Illustrated by Gini Wade

an imprint of Hodder Children's Books

Sir Walter Raleigh (1552?–1618)

1552? Walter Raleigh was born at Hayes Barton, South Devon.

1584–9 He organized expeditions to set up a new colony in America, named 'Virginia' (now North Carolina) after the Queen.

1585 He became one of Queen Elizabeth I's favourites, and was knighted.

1587 Raleigh was appointed Captain of the Queen's Guard. About a year later he secretly married Bess Throckmorton, one of the Queen's maids of honour. Elizabeth was very angry and Raleigh was banished from Court.

1588 When the Spanish Armada threatened to invade, Raleigh helped to organize England's defence.

1595 He led an expedition to South America, and travelled up the Orinoco River in search of El Dorado, the legendary 'City of Gold'.

1603 Queen Elizabeth died and James I became king. Raleigh was accused of plotting with Spain and sentenced to death but he was imprisoned in the Tower of London instead.

1616 Raleigh was released and led a second expedition to South America the following year. It was a disastrous failure.

1618 On his return he was sentenced to death on the original charge of treason. On 29 October he faced the executioner with great bravery, and even joked with him about the sharpness of his axe.

Chapter 1
Farewell to England

It was a raw February day, in the year
1595, when Ben Wharton stood looking
out over Plymouth Harbour at the great
ships anchored there. He pulled his
leather-jack tightly round his shoulders
against the biting wind.

Not far out, a three-masted galleon swung on her anchor chain. All around her, small rowing boats were taking the supplies needed for her voyage. Ben's father had been a sailor, so he guessed what they were loading: barrels of beer and vinegar, cheese and salted meat; boxes of round shot for the cannon, and bows and muskets for the soldiers.

He looked up at the tall masts with their flags flying, and felt proud that this was soon to be his ship.

Suddenly Ben felt a hand gripping his shoulder, and turned round, startled.

'You must be the new cabin boy? I'm Hugh Godwin.' The boy who spoke was a few years older than Ben. He stood grinning, then, without warning, pulled him behind a pile of barrels. 'Quick, the General's coming. We don't want to meet him yet.'

From their hiding place, they watched a group of men walking quickly past.

'That's the General,' whispered Hugh, pointing to the man at the front. He was taller than anyone else, and better dressed. 'That's Sir Walter Raleigh.'

Ben noticed his neatly trimmed beard and his rich black velvet cloak. Following Raleigh, he saw two half-naked painted Indians.

'Who are they?' he asked, amazed. 'They were speaking English.'

Hugh laughed. 'They are Raleigh's interpreters – I think that's what old Thomas called them – so the General can talk to the natives in foreign lands.'

Ben watched the two Indians climb into the rowing boat behind Raleigh.

When the boys were on board the ship, old Thomas, the master gunner, showed them where they would be sleeping. 'I hope you like rats,' he said, as he took them down below decks.

Later that day, as the ship left harbour, Ben stood watching the roofs and church towers of Plymouth disappearing over the horizon. Hugh put a hand on his shoulder. Ben was full of excitement, but he wondered when he would see his home again.

Behind Raleigh's ship were two others, following like ducks on a pond.

Chapter 2
A Sailor at Last

Early the next morning Thomas prodded the boys awake. 'Come on, you lazy vagabonds! Raleigh has ordered all the crew on deck. You'd best not keep the General waiting.'

Raleigh came out of his cabin and stood in front of the crew, his white starched ruff framing his face. When he spoke his voice had the rich Devon accent that Ben knew so well.

'We are bound for South America, men,'
shouted Raleigh, against the wind, 'to the
country of Guiana, to find the City of Gold
that the Spaniards call El Dorado. We will
travel up a great river, and beat the
Spaniards to the treasure.' A great cheer
rang out. Spain was England's deadliest
enemy.

Those first days and nights Ben was
horribly sea-sick. Hugh only laughed,
eating his greasy fish stew in front of him
and knocking the crawling weevils out of
the ship's biscuits right under his nose.

After eleven days they anchored in the
Canary Islands, to take on water. When
they set sail again, Ben was no longer ill.

'You're a sailor at last,' laughed old Thomas, and now Ben could laugh as well.

With Hugh's help, he even started to climb the tall masts, his bare feet gripping the ropes. The voyage lasted more than six long weeks. It was one clear day, when both boys were high in the rigging, that they finally heard the look-out cry 'land ahoy', and saw the coastline of a new world.

Chapter 3
The River Adventure Begins

The next morning old Thomas was busy
cleaning a cannon, and checking the wheels
of its wooden carriage. Ben had nothing to
do for once, and was standing nearby,
watching the carpenters on the beach.
They were stripping the masts and decks
off the smallest ship, to make it lighter for
the river.

'Is Sir Walter Raleigh a rich gentleman,
Thomas?' Ben asked.

'None richer, Master,' Thomas replied.
'They say he was the Queen's favourite.'

The old man chuckled. 'I've heard
that Raleigh once threw his fine cloak
over a muddy puddle, just so Queen Bess
wouldn't get her shoes wet!'

Hugh joined them from below decks, looking worried. 'Ben,' he said, 'one hundred men have been chosen for the river journey, but…you are not chosen.'

Thomas looked at their faces. 'Go and ask Raleigh,' he said. 'He's a fair man.'

'Ask Raleigh?' shouted Hugh. 'He'll put us both in irons.'

After sunset, the boys stood nervously outside the General's cabin. Hugh was just about to knock when he remembered something, and caught Ben's arm.

'Don't be worried if Raleigh's cabin seems to be on fire – and don't throw a bucket of water over him, to put him out, like one servant did! He's just…"smoking" they call it.'

Ben had heard of this strange habit of setting fire to dried leaves, called tobacco. He'd even heard that the Queen had tried it.

Hugh knocked on the panelled door.

'Come in.' Raleigh's voice was sharp and loud. The boys went in, and found the General sitting behind a table piled high with leather-bound books.

In Raleigh's hand was a long silver pipe, and clouds of strong-smelling smoke filled the cabin. The boys were amazed when a smoke-ring hovered in front of them.

'Come on lad, speak up,' Raleigh said. Hugh stammered Ben's request. And, to his amazement, Raleigh agreed.

'Your father sailed with me, Master Ben Wharton,' Raleigh said, 'and for his sake I will take you. You will be treated like a man, and you must bear all the same hardships as the other men. Do you understand?' Ben nodded.

Raleigh smiled at the boy. He was thinking of himself at Ben's age, sailing on Devon's calmer waters, and longing for adventure.

At last the larger ship, holding sixty men, and four smaller boats set out. Ben and Hugh were given the job of look-outs in the bows.

'Your eyes are young,' said one of Raleigh's captains. 'Watch for any movement. And be ready to throw the lead-line overboard, to check the river depth, whenever your captain calls.'

On the second day, Ben spotted a canoe with three natives, travelling fast upstream. 'Quick,' Raleigh ordered, 'take them captive!'

The leading boat, with eight swift oarsmen, quickly overtook the canoe. After a struggle, all three natives were captured. But Raleigh decided to take only one, an old man, with him. He would know the river well and would guide their boats through.

When they camped that night, the boys listened to Raleigh telling stories about the Golden King. 'Every morning the King's servants blow gold dust all over his body with pipes, and every night he bathes the gold away. And the golden statues in his city weigh 20 tons each.'

But old Thomas had more frightening tales, of a tribe who ate their prisoners, and another tribe whose eyes were in the middle of their shoulders. The lights from the camp-fires made strange shadows in the trees, and neither boy slept well that night.

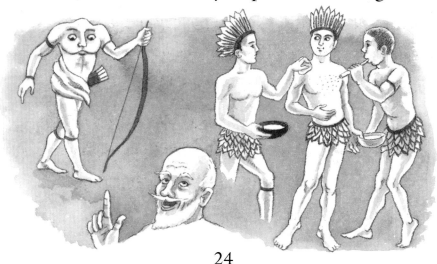

Chapter 4
River Monsters and Gold Dust

Days passed, and their water supplies had
gone. The sticky heat was terrible and they
were drenched by sudden rainstorms. They
fished, and dug in the sand for turtles'
eggs. There were coloured fruits to gather
and strange animals, like jungle pigs, to
hunt. But their only drink was the bitter
yellow river water.

The old native prisoner told them of a
village nearby where they could get clean
water, and chickens and bread, but Raleigh
did not trust him.

Two small boats set out with Raleigh.
Hugh and Ben were in the party of sailors
with him, and the General promised they
would be back by nightfall.

As the hours went by, Raleigh became angry. 'Where is this village?' he shouted at the old man, and pulled out his sword. The boys thought he was going to use it.

Night fell and there was deep darkness. The trees were so low that every touch felt like a serpent's bite, but Ben dared not show he was afraid. He had promised Raleigh.

It was after midnight when Hugh cried out, 'There are fires along the bank!' Dogs began to bark, and they realized the old man had been telling the truth.

That night they slept in the Chief's house, with full stomachs. When daylight came Ben could not believe his eyes. 'Look,' he called to Hugh, 'there are deer grazing.'

The darkness had hidden a wide valley, with grassy slopes.

Later, just as they returned to their crews, a terrible thing happened that Ben would remember all his life. A scream rang out. A native boy had fallen into the river.

'Help him!' shouted Thomas. 'Look, there are fierce water monsters!'

But no one could reach the boy in time. When their boats moved off again, the monsters' long jaws could still be seen, just beneath the surface.

As each day passed, the crew became
more frightened and disheartened. Their
scouts still saw no sign of the mountains
of Guiana, nor of the Golden City. Even
Raleigh could not encourage the men
any more.

But one morning, as the boats rounded a bend in the river, four canoes appeared, rowing fast. Some of the men were dressed in Spanish uniforms. The canoes rammed the bank, and all the men disappeared into the trees.

'Captain Gifford,' Raleigh shouted, 'after them, with soldiers.'

Eight soldiers with muskets leapt ashore and chased into the forest. From the river, gunfire could be heard.

After some time the soldiers returned, and one of them handed Raleigh a small basket. Raleigh emptied it carefully on the bank.

Hugh was closer than Ben. 'There are bottles and weighing scales,' he said, 'and some kind of powder.'

Raleigh smiled as he held the bottles up. 'These are for testing gold,' he said. He tipped a small heap of the powder onto his hand, and even in the dull light it shone like the sun.

'Now my hand is covered with gold,' he said, 'just like the Golden King.' Raleigh's eyes sparkled with new hope. It seemed the trail was warm.

'And look at this,' shouted old Thomas. In the bottom of one of the canoes he had found loaves of delicious bread, which perhaps pleased the hungry sailors even more.

It happened that same afternoon, just as the boats were tying up by the shore. Ben's foot slipped on the wet woodwork, the boat dipped a little, and he overbalanced into the evil-smelling water. Hugh was in the boat and saw a movement from the far bank.

'Ben,' he shouted, 'watch out for the monsters!' Scarcely were the words out of his mouth than he had leapt in to rescue his friend. It took but a moment before Captain Gifford and old Thomas were hauling them both back on board. Ben lay in the bottom of the boat, coughing and spluttering for breath, but unharmed. Neither boy noticed the long snout touching the side of their boat.

Chapter 5
Topiawari's Feast

When Ben woke the next morning, he had overslept and Hugh's hammock was empty. He saw him near the river bank with two men. One was an older sailor. And, to Ben's surprise, the other man, with his back turned, was Raleigh.

'Trouble?' said Ben, when Hugh returned, but his friend would say nothing.

There was excitement in the camp that day. News of Raleigh's coming had spread through the forest, from tribe to tribe, and a great Chief called Topiawari invited Raleigh and his men to a feast. Leaving just a few sailors to guard their boats, they walked to the Chief's village.

There was more food and wine than they could have imagined: joints of venison, chicken and fish, and a strange juicy fruit, called a pina, that they had never seen before.

Old Thomas had too much wine to drink, and his voice grew louder. 'The Chief is even older than me,' he shouted to Ben. 'He is 110 years old.'

Raleigh sat with Topiawari inside a tent, and asked the old man how close they were to the kingdom of gold. 'Just four days journey,' he replied, 'but the mighty River Orinoco is against you.'

Raleigh left the feast and walked to the river bank. He watched the thundering water, and he knew he was beaten. When he returned, his men could see it in his face.

He walked up to Chief Topiawari.

'I come from a great queen across the seas,' he said. From his purse he took a golden sovereign with Queen Elizabeth's face on it. He gave it to the Chief as a gift. 'Next year we will return, and with your help we will find the City of Gold.'

In return the old man gave Raleigh the oddest beast.

'It has plates of armour on its body, Hugh,' Ben laughed. But Hugh was strangely silent.

40

On the river bank Raleigh's crew and all
the tribesmen had gathered, and Topiawari
spoke. 'Take my son with you to your
queen, as a sign of our friendship.' A young
man stepped forward and stood next to
Raleigh.

Then Raleigh spoke. 'And I leave with
you a brave sailor, and also a brave English
boy who is nearly a man.'

Ben could not believe it when Hugh walked towards him. Hugh grasped Ben's hand, but neither boy could find words to speak. He then stood with the older sailor, next to the Chief.

As the boats were drawn into the fierce current, Raleigh stood with his hand raised in farewell. Ben's hand was also raised as he watched the two figures standing on the bank, until a bend of the river removed them from his sight.

Chapter 6

How the Story Ended

It was not until the year 1617, more than twenty years later, that Sir Walter Raleigh was able to keep his word and return to the country of Guiana.

The old Queen had died in 1603, and the new King, James, was sour and spiteful. He listened to Raleigh's enemies and Raleigh was soon accused of plotting with Spain, and found guilty of treason. But, instead of being executed, he spent thirteen years as a prisoner in the Tower of London.

At last, when he had almost given up hope, he was allowed one more voyage. He could return to the lands of South America and search again for their golden treasures. But his health was broken, the voyage was a disaster, and his beloved son Wat was killed.

On his return to England Raleigh was put on trial again, and sentenced to death. He spent the night before his execution entertaining his friends, laughing and joking, then said his last goodbyes to his faithful wife Bess.

And what happened to Hugh Godwin? Sadly, within a few weeks of being left behind, Hugh is said to have been killed by wild animals in the forest. But one legend says he survived. We shall never know for certain.

And Ben Wharton grew up to be an officer in the King's Navy. Like Raleigh, he sailed the oceans of the world, but always returned to his beloved Devon, and remembered the great man he had served when he was a boy.

Glossary

galleon a large sailing ship in Elizabethan times

interpreters people who can change one language to another

lead-line a line with a heavy metal weight to check the water's depth

leather-jack a sleeveless coat made of leather

master gunner seaman in charge of the sailors firing the cannon

pina pineapple

Queen Bess a nickname for Queen Elizabeth I

ruff a starched linen collar, very fashionable at this time

serpent a snake

ship's biscuits a bread-like substance, made from very hard baked wheat and barley

sovereign a gold coin worth one pound

vagabonds people without work; beggars

venison deer meat

weevils small beetles which eat their way into sacks of grain and food